DISTRICT 13

BEFORE THE SNAP

Katherine Hengel

SADDLEBACK
EDUCATIONAL PUBLISHING

DISTRICT 13

SADDLEBACK
EDUCATIONAL PUBLISHING
www.sdlback.com

ISBN-13: 978-1-61651-581-2
ISBN-10: 1-61651-581-3
eBook: 978-1-61247-246-1

Printed in Guangzhou, China
NOR/0713/CA21301346

17 16 15 14 13   4 5 6 7 8

Taras got off the bus. Derrick
followed. He was moving slowly. His
leg was sore.

"You gonna make it?" Taras
asked.

"Huh?" Derrick replied.

"My grandma gets off the bus
faster than you."

Derrick put his backpack on. "She
a receiver? She after my JV spot?"

"Forget about grandma," Taras said. "Worry about *Colton*. That fool wants blood. He's trying to take you out, man."

"For real," Derrick said. He shook his head. "Cheap shots. All the time. He's messing up my legs. I swear. Guess he's sick of seeing me start."

They walked down the block. It was a cool, fall day. School had just started. The boys had practice after school. They were on their way home.

"Know what gets to Colton more? Than seeing you start?" Taras asked.

"What's that?"

"His girl staring at you," Taras said.

Derrick tried not to smile. But he couldn't help it. He had to! Taras was right. Tasheka was eyeing him. Derrick didn't know why. She was cool and popular. He was always nervous. And he got bad grades. Still, he liked her attention.

"She's not his girl anymore. Right?"

"That's right! She's his *old* girl. So when you two gonna hook up? When you gonna ask her out?"

Derrick shook his head. "I just got done with one cheerleader. Remember? I don't need another one."

Taras rolled his eyes. "Come on. That was kid stuff. Amber Linn was like a little sister. Not a hookup."

Derrick didn't like talking about Amber Linn. "You don't get it, T."

"Lose the nerves, Derrick. Tasheka likes you. She's single. You're single. She's hot! Ask her out. Enjoy it! What's wrong with you?"

Derrick didn't answer.

Derrick's leg hurt. Going up stairs was hard. Too bad he lived on the third floor. He took each step slowly. Colton really hit him hard.

Derrick's mom was home. She was putting on lipstick. Derrick rolled his eyes. "You seeing *him*?" he asked.

"*Him*?" she replied. She didn't like his comment. Not one bit. "You mean *John*? The first man I've seen in five years? Since your father left? Then, yes. I am going to see *him*."

Derrick dropped his backpack on the floor. He walked to his room. He'd met John a couple of times. He wasn't impressed. He was too polished. What did he want from his mom?

Derrick sat on his bed. He had to look at his leg. He pulled his jeans down. Yep. There it was. One hell of bruise.

Derrick heard the phone ring. His mom answered it. Derrick was sure it was John. John the bank teller.

His mom knocked. "Derrick? It's for you," she said. Derrick pulled up his pants. He opened the door.

"Who is it?" he asked.

Something was wrong. He could tell by his mom's face.

"It's Linny, baby."

Derrick's heart sank. Forget about his leg. Now his heart hurt.

"Want me to wait?" his mom whispered. "Until you get off the phone? I'm sure John wouldn't mind …"

Derrick held out his hand. "Go," he said. His heart was racing. He hadn't talked to Amber Linn since they broke up.

"Good luck, baby," his mom said. She left. Derrick took a deep breath.

"Linny?"

"Hey, Derrick."

"How are you?" he asked.

She was silent. Derrick couldn't take it.

"Linny?"

Amber Linn started to cry. Derrick felt terrible. He cared about Amber Linn. Always had. Always would.

"Linny, stop crying and …"

"I have something to tell you," she said. "It's big, Derrick. It happened right after we broke up."

"What? What happened?"

"I swear Derrick. It was *after* we broke up. I …"

Derrick heard her inhale.

"I'm pregnant. You don't know the guy."

Now the pain moved to his stomach. It wasn't possible. How

could it be? With some other guy? They just broke up a couple of months ago.

Derrick sat on his bed. He felt sick. He couldn't speak. He didn't know what to say.

"Everyone will think it's your baby, Derrick. If they find out it isn't, then …"

That didn't sound right. Derrick was in shock. But he wasn't deaf. He forced himself to focus. "What do you mean, *if*?"

"I'm going to look like a huge slut. Everyone will know."

"Know what, Linny? What are you getting at?"

"That I … was with someone right after you."

Derrick moved the phone to his other ear. This was unbelievable. What did she expect him to do? He ran his free hand over his face.

"That *is* the truth, Linny. Right?"

Amber Linn began to cry again. Harder than before. She could barely breathe.

"Linny, I'm sorry. But what do you..."

"I just had to tell you, okay? I had to tell *someone*. I'm scared, Derrick."

Amber Linn was sobbing now. Derrick could barely understand her. "Linny, calm down. Nobody knows?"

"Nobody."

"Not even your mom?"

"Of course not. My dad doesn't

know either. In case you were wondering."

Derrick knew Amber Linn. He knew she was alone in this. Just like she said. She hadn't seen her father in years. They had that in common.

"Linny, I'm sure ..."

"Look, Derrick. I'm thinking about my options. I don't know what to do. I just ... had to tell you. I don't know why. Don't tell anyone, okay?"

"Yes. I mean no. I mean, I won't tell anyone."

Derrick was a mess at practice the next day. He forgot his routes. He dropped passes. Amber Linn's news really upset him.

Of course, Colton was thrilled. "What's the matter, Big D? Can't hang onto the ball today?"

Derrick blew him off. He knew he was better than Colton. He always would be. Even on an off day.

Coach called the next play. Derrick was to run across the middle. Colton would cover him.

Derrick stood at the line. Colton was across from him. "Focus," he told himself. "Just run your route and focus."

The center snapped the ball. Derrick ran up the field. He looked over his shoulder. He saw the pass. It was right there. He ran to meet the ball. He had this one. He knew it.

He was wrong. Colton saw Derrick would make the catch. He tackled him from behind. Derrick fell to the ground. It was an obvious penalty.

The whistle blew. Colton jumped up. He tried to defend his actions.

Derrick rolled over onto his back. Another cheap shot. He didn't even have the strength to fight about it. Not today anyway.

He stared up at the sky. It was clouding up. A raindrop hit his cheek. He only wanted one thing. He wanted to go home.

After practice, Coach said, "Got a minute, Derrick?"

"I'll catch you out front," Taras said. Derrick nodded. He walked over to Coach.

"Derrick, I see Colton's cheap shots. You know that. Right?" Derrick nodded.

"I'm proud of you. Keep ignoring him. I'll take care of it. Okay? You hear me?"

"Yes, sir," Derrick said. Coach slapped him on the back. Then Derrick met Taras by the door.

"Everything okay?" Taras asked.

"Coach told me to ignore Colton. Said he'll deal with him."

They stepped out into the rain. Taras slapped Derrick's shoulder. "It's about time! Colton's a punk. You wanna stop at Micky D's? Get a burger?"

"Nah. I just want to go home," Derrick admitted.

They walked to the bus stop. It was really pouring now. Someone was in the bus shelter. It was Tasheka.

Tasheka shivered in her cheerleading clothes. It was cold and windy. When Tasheka saw them, she smiled. "Hi, Taras, Derrick," she said.

"This ain't your stop," Derrick replied.

"I know *that*," Tasheka said. She smiled again.

Taras went into the shelter. Derrick stayed outside. Rain dripped down his face.

"It's just such a nice night," Tasheka joked. "Thought I'd take the 33. You know. Walk a few extra blocks."

The bus pulled up. They all got on. Two girls were sitting in the middle. Tasheka, Taras, and Derrick sat in back.

"So, Derrick. How was practice?" Tasheka asked.

"All right," Derrick said. Then he just stared out the window. Tasheka was confused. She wished Derrick would talk to her.

Taras stepped in. "Derrick took some cheap hits today. Right, D?"

"Yeah, that's right. Just like every day."

Tasheka felt awkward. Taras did too. They all sat in silence. Tasheka got off at the next stop.

"What the hell is wrong with you?" Taras yelled.

Derrick watched Tasheka pull up her hood. She walked with her head down.

"Derrick, are you high or something? What is going on?" Taras asked.

"Linny's pregnant, Taras. That's what's going on."

Taras leaned back. "Damn. That's messed up. Is it … *yours*?"

"Hell, no," Derrick said.

"But how did she, you know. So fast? Whose is it?"

"How the hell should I know? I just know it's Linny's. She's fourteen, man. *Fourteen*. Don't tell anyone. Not *anyone*. You feel me, man?"

"No problem, D. I won't say anything."

The bus lurched to a stop again. The two girls hopped off. The doors closed and the bus pulled away.

"Oh, my God! Can you believe she's pregnant?" one girl said to the other.

"I know! I can't wait to tell Brandi!"

Word spread about Amber Linn the next day. News like that travels. *Fast*. By the end of the day, everyone knew.

Derrick walked into the locker room. Colton greeted him. "It's Daddy Derrick! Welcome to practice!"

Derrick glared at Taras. "Thanks, T. Thanks a lot. Way to keep a secret," he said.

Taras looked confused. He tried to speak. But Derrick wouldn't listen. He slammed his locker door. He walked to the field.

The team stretched and warmed up. They formed groups and did some drills. Derrick was in his own world. He was there. But he wasn't.

What would Amber Linn do? Would she have the baby? Would she give it away? It wasn't Derrick's problem. But it felt like it was.

"First string offense. Let's run it," Coach yelled.

Derrick lined up with the offense. He stood across from Colton.

"You look tired, D. How you sleeping? Not ready to be a daddy, huh?"

Derrick reached across the line. He grabbed Colton's jersey. "I'm gonna be *your* daddy, fool. You best shut that mouth."

Coach blew the whistle. Taras got in between Derrick and Colton. But Derrick wasn't done. He pointed at Colton. "You remember what I said. I ain't playin'!" he yelled.

"Damn it, Derrick. Get over here," Coach yelled. "Henderson, go in for Derrick."

Coach pulled Derrick off the field. He was not impressed. "Sit down, Derrick. What the hell's gotten into you? That how you ignore a punk?"

Derrick sat on the bench. The offense started a play. Coach put his hands on his hips. "Listen to me,

Derrick. Be a man. Do what you gotta do. Understand? A baby isn't the end of the world.

Come back tomorrow with a clear head. Okay? Now carry these tires in. Go."

Derrick wanted to tell Coach the truth. But he didn't know how. He was too angry to explain. So he picked up two tires. He stormed off the field.

Derrick carried the tires inside. It was a long way. He was sweaty and full of rage.

In the storage room, he threw one tire into the wall. It hit with a thud. He threw the other tire. Bang!

Derrick heard the door open. He was sure it was Coach. His stomach dropped. Coach would not like the tire throwing.

But it wasn't Coach. It was Tasheka. "I need to talk to you," she said. She didn't look happy.

The door slammed behind her. "You were rude to me yesterday," she said. "I just want to get to know you. All right?"

Derrick was breathing heavily. The storage room was hot and small. There wasn't much light. And Tasheka was so close. He tried to catch his breath.

"I saw you snap on Colton," she said. She moved closer. "Is my ex too much for you? Is he why you're ignoring me?"

Tasheka pointed at Derrick. The other hand went on her hip. "Because if you can't handle …"

"I can handle it," Derrick said. He moved closer. Tasheka looked nervous. But he didn't stop. Soon his chest hit her finger.

The door opened again.

"What are you kids up to? Get the hell out of here!" It was a janitor. Derrick and Tasheka ran.

6

"That old fool scared me!" Tasheka
said. She was out of breath. They
were in an empty hall.

"Girl, I was at top speed. You kept
right up with me. You going out for
track in the spring?"

Tasheka laughed. "Oh, hell no.
Spring is for the sun. Not running."

Derrick smiled. Tasheka really
was cool.

"Look, Tasheka. I'm sorry about yesterday. You know. On the bus. I just … have a lot on my mind."

Tasheka nodded. "Is it Amber Linn?"

Derrick froze. Did Tasheka know about the baby?

"What do you mean?"

"I mean is there anything between you two?"

Derrick was relieved. She must not know. He relaxed. "No. It's over. I mean, I look out for her. Like a sister. That's it. I swear."

Tasheka touched Derrick's cheek. "I'm happy to hear that," she whispered. "But I gotta go. Can't be late for dinner. I'll hit you up tomorrow, okay?"

On the bus ride home, Derrick's mind raced. He wanted to tell Tasheka the truth. Would she understand? That this baby thing was just a misunderstanding?

No. Tasheka was cool. But not *that* cool. Derrick had to talk to Amber Linn. He couldn't lie anymore.

At home, Derrick called Amber Linn. She wasn't happy to hear from him.

"Linny. I need to talk to you. I'm taking heat at practice. Coach talked to me about manning up. Taking care of the baby. I can't do this. I can't lie about it. You feel me?"

"Know what I feel, Derrick? Angry. Angry that you had to tell the whole school I'm pregnant. What the hell? Why did you do that?"

Derrick was furious. "Why did *you* get pregnant?"

Silence.

"I'm sure you already forgot. But let me remind you, Derrick," Amber Linn said. "You broke up with me. Remember? I wasn't feeling the greatest."

Derrick's heart stopped. There it was. The guilt. He'd felt it since he broke things off. He knew he hurt her. He knew Linny. She didn't have a lot of confidence. Or a lot of friends.

It had always been the two of them. He worried about her after the breakup. He didn't know what she would do. Now he knew.

"Tell Coach whatever the hell you want," Amber Linn said. Then she hung up.

7

Derrick was so tired that night. But
he couldn't sleep. He tossed and
turned. He could hear a baby crying
on the second floor. It made him
think of Amber Linn.

In the morning, he woke up still
tired. He went into the kitchen.

His mom was there. "Hey, baby,"
she said. "Everything okay? With
Linny?"

"She's fine," Derrick lied. He wanted to tell her. Maybe she would know what Amber Linn should do. After all, she got pregnant young too.

"I'm happy to hear that. I worry about that girl. You know? You two were always so close. Peas in a pod."

Derrick couldn't take it. Even school would be better than this. "I gotta go, Ma," he said.

But Derrick was wrong. School was *not* better. He arrived to find Tasheka at his locker. It was just before first period. The hallway was packed.

"Nothing between you two, huh?" she yelled. "Nothing except a *baby*?"

Everyone stopped and stared. No one was about to miss this.

"Is it yours? Is it?"

Derrick felt trapped. He didn't know what to do. If he told the truth, he'd hurt Linny. If he lied, he'd hurt Tasheka.

He opened his locker. Tasheka slammed the door closed. "Let's hear it, Derrick. Let's hear the truth."

Derrick slapped the locker with his hand. "What do you want, Tasheka? Want me to *abandon* her? Would that make you happy?"

Derrick pushed through the crowd. He knew exactly where he was going. The library. Amber Linn had study hall there first period. He had to talk to her.

He snuck in just before the bell rang. He saw Amber Linn sitting near a bookshelf. He hid behind it. She didn't see him.

The monitor took attendance. Then he started chatting with the tech guy. This was Derrick's chance.

"Psst! Linny!"

Amber Linn looked up from her book. She saw Derrick. She looked back down.

"*Linny!*"

Several other people looked up. Amber Linn had to respond. She stood up. She walked around the shelf. She pretended to look for a book. She went over to Derrick.

"What do you want?" she whispered.

"Linny, I know I hurt you. I'm sorry. I am. Do you believe me? I've

never been so sorry about anything.
I hope you believe me. I care about
you. I always will."

Amber Linn stared down at the
floor.

"Damn it, Amber Linn. You hurt
me too, you know. Who is this guy?
Who was he to you?"

"I told you before. You don't know
him."

"Come on. I've known you all your
life. How could you know anyone I
don't?"

Amber Linn looked Derrick in the
eye. "I can't tell you, okay? Just let it
go. Please?"

Derrick looked up at the ceiling.
He didn't feel ready for this. Not
even close.

"All right. Whatever you say, Linny. But listen. Whoever this guy is, he should be helping you. And here's another thing. I'm not lying about this. Don't ask me to. I'm not taking his heat another second."

Derrick turned and walked to the door.

Amber Linn leaned against the shelf. She started to cry. She wasn't ready for this either.

8

Derrick left the library. It was still first period. He couldn't stay in the hall. So he went into the bathroom.

He looked in the mirror. Focus, he told himself. Just like running a route. Then the bell rang. He needed to see Tasheka.

Derrick found her at her locker. She looked so mad. Like she wanted to chew him up.

"Tasheka, can I talk to you?"

"Back off," she spat.

"I want to tell you the truth. Will you let me?"

Tasheka laughed. "You don't know how to tell the truth. Maybe you can teach your own baby better."

Tasheka walked into class. The room was right next to her locker. Derrick saw her sit down. To hell with it. He was going to tell her the truth. No matter what she said.

He entered the classroom. He stood in front of her desk.

"Here's the truth, Tasheka. I don't know whose baby it is."

She leaned back in her chair. "Oh? But you know you're not the daddy?"

"That's right."

"And how are you so sure?"

Derrick put his hands on her desk. "Because I never had sex with nobody!" he yelled. "That good enough for you?"

9

The rest of the day was rough for
Derrick. He tried to keep his head
down. But he was the talk of the
school.

He could feel everyone's eyes on
him. He knew the whispers were
about him. He hated it.

Taras caught up to him at lunch.
Man, Derrick was happy to see him!
Taras wouldn't judge him.

They stood in the cafeteria line. Today was taco day. They carried their trays to a corner table. They sat down.

"Sounds like you've been busy. Busting into study hall. Yelling in classrooms," Taras said.

Derrick smiled. "Yeah, that's about right."

"Hey, man. I want you to know. I didn't tell anyone. About Amber Linn. Those girls on the bus must have heard us."

"No worries," Derrick said. "Maybe Linny told someone herself. Who knows? That girl ain't thinking straight."

"What happened in the library? She tell you who the daddy is?"

"No," Derrick said. "She said she can't tell me. Like I'd be too mad or something."

10

Derrick made it through the day.
Barely. During fifth period, he
thought about skipping. But he had
study hall with Coach sixth period.
So he stuck it out. He even made it
to practice.

The team warmed up with
drills. Then they lined up. Derrick
stood across from Colton, as usual.
Derrick's day had been so bad. Not

even Colton could make things worse.

"Hey man, sorry for that daddy stuff yesterday."

Derrick didn't know what to say. It took him a minute. "Don't worry about it," he finally replied.

Colton wasn't finished. "I mean, you *couldn't* be the daddy. Being a virgin and all. So that must mean *I'm* the daddy!"

Derrick stared at him. Amber Linn would never. Or would she?

Colton continued, "I was happy to let you take the heat. But I can't now! Damn, thanks a lot, D!"

Just then the center snapped the ball. But Derrick didn't run his route. He grabbed Colton's facemask instead. He twisted with all his might. Colton was on the ground in seconds. Derrick punched him.

Taras and Coach looked at each other. Neither moved a muscle. Derrick kept punching Colton. Colton fought back. They rolled around on the ground.

Finally Coach and the center pulled them apart. "Okay, boys. That's enough," Coach said. "That's enough."

Derrick stood still. He was breathing hard. Coach looked at him. He knew what was going on. He heard Colton's confession.

Coach didn't want to send Derrick away. But Derrick started the fight. He had to face the consequences.

"Hit the showers and go home, Derrick," he said.

Derrick walked back to school. He tried hard not to cry. He was just so sad. Sad for Linny. Sad that telling the truth only made things worse.

Derrick heard someone behind him. He turned around. It was Tasheka. She was out of breath. "Can I walk with you?" she panted.

Derrick looked across the field. The other cheerleaders were still practicing. "Aren't you supposed to be at practice?"

"I saw you and Colton going at it. Then I saw you leaving," she said. "So I, uh, acted sick."

"Then you sprinted across two football fields?"

Tasheka smiled. "Like I told you in the storage room. I'm just trying to get to know you. Okay?"

Now Derrick smiled too. Tasheka really was cool as hell. He held out his hand. Tasheka took it. They walked into school together.